To the winged white Knight
who saved me from the Dragon
D. P.

For Carole, Louise, Katie, Emily,
Amelia and Elizabeth Alice
W. A.

ISBN: 0-307-17500-6   A MCMXCIII

Library of Congress Cataloging-in-Publication Data

Passes, David.
Dragons. : truth, myth, and legend / written by David Passes ;
illustrated by Wayne Anderson.
p.   cm.
Summary: Presents various myths and legends about
dragons and discusses dragon lore from around the world.
ISBN 0-307-17500-6 : $14.95
1. Dragons—Juvenile literature.
[1. Dragons—Folklore. 2. Folklore. 3. Mythology.]
I. Anderson, Wayne. ill. II. Title.
GR830.D7P37 1993
398.2—dc20   92-44745
CIP   AC

DRAGONS
Truth, Myth, and Legend

WRITTEN BY DAVID PASSES

ILLUSTRATED BY WAYNE ANDERSON

GOLDEN BOOKS
WESTERN PUBLISHING COMPANY, INC.
850 THIRD AVENUE
NEW YORK, NEW YORK 10022

INTRODUCTION

Just a few hundred years ago, sightings of dragons were quite common. Ordinary people saw them; so did kings, knights, archbishops, and monks. Scholars wrote about them.

It was only about 400 years ago, when scientists began the enormous task of identifying all the known animals, that anyone even began to doubt the existence of dragons. Today most scientists say that dragons never existed. There is simply no proof. So what exactly were the dragons that people claimed to see?

First of all, it must be remembered that scientific understanding was not the same then as it is today. If the sky rumbled with thunder, and was then filled with flashes of lightning, someone might easily believe that a dragon was flying by. Or if a wandering traveler saw smoke and fire belching from a distant volcano, what else could it be but a dragon?

Imagine Marco Polo in the thirteenth century, the first European to travel overland to the Far East, as he came across a crocodile for the first time. His description—and an artist's rendering made at the time—was exactly like a dragon. Or suppose someone found gigantic footprints or fossilized bones long before the facts about dinosaurs were understood. It is no wonder that people could believe in dragons.

Many present-day lizards look very dragonlike. Most of them are small, but there is a type of giant lizard that was discovered on the Indonesian island of Komodo in 1912. It grows up to nine feet long and stands three feet high. It feeds mostly on goats, pigs, and deer, but it is known to have eaten humans. Its saliva is poisonous and its breath more foul than that of any other creature on Earth. It lays eggs and has a forked tongue. Naturally, this lizard is known as the Komodo dragon. Although it is not the winged dragon of fame and legend, it does give hope to those who still want to believe that dragons live!

Frontispiece
A legendary **Heraldic dragon**. These were the dragons that supposedly held princesses captive, hoarded treasure, and were eventually defeated by heroes and saints. They were said to live in lakes, marshes, mountains, and burial mounds. A mature dragon could be any size between 23 and 230 feet long.

CONTENTS

MARDUK AND TIAMAT

This story of the creation was recorded on clay tablets
nearly 4,000 years ago in the city of Babylon.

In the beginning there was nothing—no Earth, no sky, no gods, no people. Only Apsu and Tiamat. Apsu was male, the spirit of fresh water and emptiness. Tiamat was female, the spirit of salt water and chaos; she was a dragon. Together Apsu and Tiamat contained the seeds of all living things, and their children became the gods.

One of their children, Ea, had the power to know the future. He was so great and strong that Apsu decided to destroy him. Of course, Ea knew about Apsu's plan, because he knew the future. So to save himself, he tied Apsu up and killed him.

Tiamat was furious. She decided to kill Ea. Ea, who knew already that Tiamat would defeat him, held a meeting with the other gods. They decided to ask Marduk, the most powerful god of all, to battle Tiamat. He alone would stand a chance against her. Marduk said yes, but on one condition: If he won, he would be lord over all the universe.

Marduk and Tiamat prepared for battle. Marduk armed himself with a net and a club, and a bow that fired arrows of lightning. He rode a chariot pulled by four fierce horses with the four winds to accompany them. Tiamat created horrible monsters to fight by her side—demon lions, savage dogs, scorpion men, and eleven glittering dragons.

The fight began. Marduk spread his net to capture Tiamat. Quickly she opened her mouth wide to swallow Marduk. Seeing his chance, Marduk sent one of his winds inside her. It blasted down her throat and blew her jaws apart. Marduk drew his bow and fired an arrow through her gaping mouth straight into her heart. Then he hurled his net over Tiamat's fleeing horde of monsters and put them in chains. Victorious, he split Tiamat's body into two halves. From one half he made the heavens and from the other he made the Earth. From the blood of one of the chained monsters he made people and placed them on Earth to serve the gods.

And so order was made from chaos
and the world was formed.

INDRA AND VRITRA

For centuries the people of India sang a hymn about Indra and Vritra before the story was written down in about 1200 B.C. Water was so precious in those times that the god who controlled it was thought to be all-powerful.

Long ago, before the world was fully formed, Indra was the god of all warriors. He was also the god of nature and the bringer of rain. But he had one enemy, Vritra, a mighty, limbless dragon that crawled over the mountaintops and held all the waters of heaven in his belly. Indra had to destroy Vritra before the waters could flow upon Earth. Indra got ready to fight Vritra. He took the sun for his chariot and thunderbolts for his arrows. Then he charged on his enemy. But Vritra saw him coming and attacked first. Vritra was a ferocious opponent. For a while, Indra seemed to be losing the fight, as the huge serpent wound about him in suffocating coils.

Then Vritra made a big mistake.
For one brief moment, he took his eyes
off his victim. Indra saw his chance to win.
Quick as a flash, he fired one of his thunderbolts.
It struck Vritra in the heart and killed him.

As he rolled, lifeless, down the mountainside,
the great dragon burst apart, releasing the heavenly
waters. Rivers gushed and tumbled down to make the sea.
Indra's sun chariot rose in the sky, and the first dawn broke
over a new world.

HERACLES AND THE HYDRA

Heracles, sometimes called Hercules, is a hero of Classical legends.
This is one of many stories about him.

Heracles was the human son of Zeus, king of the gods, and was born with supernatural strength. While still a baby, he strangled some serpents that tried to kill him in his cradle. As a boy, he killed a lion that attacked his family's herds of sheep.

Like many young men, Heracles married and became a father. But one day, in a terrible fit of madness, he killed all his children. Horrified by what he had done, Heracles ran away to a place called Argolis. There, Eurystheus, the ruler of Greece, ordered Heracles to do twelve nearly impossible labors as punishment for his crime. One of these was to kill the Hydra, a dragon with nine heads.

Each night the Hydra left its murky den in the swamps to massacre animals and ruin the crops of the local farmers. But every time someone tried to kill the Hydra, they failed. As soon as they chopped off one of its heads, another just grew in its place. Not only that, the breath of the Hydra was so poisonous that anyone who breathed its fumes immediately fell down and died.

With his friend Iolaus, Heracles set out to kill the Hydra. Soon they came to a spring of clear, fresh water. Somewhere nearby, the Hydra lay hiding.

Heracles shot several flaming arrows into the air to bring the Hydra out in the open. As it crawled closer to him, the eyes blazed in each of its nine horrible heads. Heracles held his breath and raised his heavy club.

Down came the club and knocked off one of the Hydra's heads. The dragon roared with rage as Heracles brought down the club again and again. But each time a head fell off, another grew back in its place.

To Heracles the task seemed impossible. "What can I do?" he called to his friend.

Iolaus knew what to do. He lit a torch and thrust it into Heracles' hand. "Each time you strike off a head," he shouted, "scorch the stump with this flame!"

With renewed strength, Heracles returned to battle. *Whack!* A head fell. *Sssst!* The flame sizzled against the bloody stump. One by one the heads fell. None grew back. The Hydra was defeated.

The last of the Hydra's heads was believed to be immortal, so Heracles buried it beneath a giant rock, where it could cause no harm.

Then he dipped his arrows in the Hydra's poisonous blood.

He would be well armed for future adventures.

CADMUS AND THE GOLDEN DRAGON

The Greek hero Cadmus founded the royal city of
Thebes, where many of the Classical legends take place.

When the king of Phoenicia's daughter disappeared, he sent
his son Cadmus to search the world for her. But though he and his
companions traveled far and wide, Cadmus failed to find his sister. So he
went to the famous Oracle at Delphi to ask what he should do. The Oracle's
advice puzzled Cadmus. She advised him to forget about his sister, for he
would never see her again. She told him to follow a sacred cow that he
would find outside the temple. He was to follow the cow until she lay down
to rest. On that spot he was to build a city.

Cadmus and his companions did as they were told and followed the cow
as she wandered over the hills. At last she lay down in a circle of shady trees.
The thirsty travelers could hear the refreshing sounds of a nearby spring.
Cadmus sent his companions to fetch water. He sat on the soft grass and
waited and waited, but his friends never returned. After a while Cadmus
went to see what had become of them. Close to the spring, he found them.
They were all dead, their bodies torn and covered with blood. Cadmus looked
up to see drops of blood dripping to the ground. Towering over him was a
huge golden dragon with three rows of razor-sharp teeth.

Instantly Cadmus drew back his spear and plunged it far into the monster's flesh. To his horror, it did not die. Instead the creature uncoiled and moved toward him, fire flaring from its nostrils, its sharp teeth gleaming. Cadmus fell back as the creature attacked.

Cornered and desperate, Cadmus thrust his spear past the triple rows of teeth, deep into the dragon's belly. Black blood spewed from the monster's mouth as it twisted and convulsed in pain. But before it could make one last frenzied attack, Cadmus heaved up an enormous rock and crushed the creature's skull.

Then Cadmus heard a voice in his head say, "Plant the teeth of the dragon you have slain." So he wrenched the teeth from the creature's gaping jaws, plowed up a field, and buried the teeth. At once the ground started to heave, and from the earth sprouted a crop of fully armed soldiers! Cadmus was afraid the soldiers would attack him, so he tossed several stones to confuse them and make them turn on one another. They fought so furiously that soon only five were left alive. One of them said, "Brothers, stop! Before all is lost, we must end this foolish bloodshed and change our fate." So they laid down their weapons and accepted Cadmus as their new leader.

The next day they buried Cadmus' friends and held a meeting. Together they pledged to help Cadmus build his city, as the Oracle had told him to do. The city, called Thebes, became great. Cadmus ruled over it for many years.

PRINCE SIGURD AND THE DRAGON FAFNIR

This Northern myth was told in verse by traveling storytellers long before it was written down in the thirteenth century.

Prince Sigurd had a powerful sword. It had been given to his father by Odin, god of wisdom and war. The prince planned to use the sword to slay a mighty dragon named Fafnir. The dragon lived in a dark cave, surrounded by a glittering hoard of treasure.

Sigurd's guardian, an evil dwarf named Reginn, was greedy for the treasure in Fafnir's cave. Reginn hoped and schemed that both the dragon and Sigurd would die so that he could have all the treasure for himself.

The prince and Reginn set off for the dragon's cave. Pressed into the earth in front of it were enormous fresh footprints. Sigurd felt a stab of fear. Fafnir was far larger than he had expected.

Now Reginn laid his evil plan. He told Sigurd to dig a deep pit beside the path to the river, where the dragon crawled each day to drink at dawn. He said, "Then hide in the pit and wait for Fafnir to come."

As Sigurd dug, an old man mysteriously appeared and spoke to him. "Young Prince," he said, "you must dig a shallow pit by the side of the deep one you dig now. Crawl into the shallow pit when Fafnir's blood begins to flow, so you will be safe from its burning power. Be warned, for though your guardian knows the blood is deadly, he did not tell you."

Before Sigurd could respond, the man vanished. Sigurd believed that the old man was the god Odin in disguise, so he dug the second pit as he had been told.

In the cool dawn Sigurd crouched in the deep pit, his sword poised ready to plunge. The ground shuddered as Fafnir lumbered toward the river. Sigurd held his breath. Then, as the dragon passed over the pit, Sigurd thrust the sword deep into its body. As the burning blood began to pour from the dragon, Sigurd slid safely away from it into the shallow pit. Fafnir writhed in pain and lashed out with its head and tail. But the wound was fatal and soon Fafnir died.

Although surprised to see that Sigurd still lived, Reginn ran to congratulate the prince. "Cook me the dragon's heart," he said, "and I shall eat it in your honor." As Sigurd cooked the heart, some of the juices ran onto his hands. Without thinking, Sigurd licked his fingers. Suddenly he could understand the language of the birds. He listened in amazement as they told him that if he ate the heart himself, he would become the wisest of men. Then the birds told Sigurd that Reginn was planning right then and there to kill him and steal all the treasure for himself.

So Sigurd swung his powerful sword once more and chopped off Reginn's head. Sigurd ate the dragon's heart and became the wisest of men. And he claimed the treasure he had so bravely fought for.

BEOWULF AND THE FIRE DRAGON

Storytellers from Northern Europe told about the exploits of the great hero Beowulf. His adventures were first written down in English by an unknown poet in the eighth century.

 Beowulf the brave had slain three terrible monsters in his youth. Since then he had become king of the Geats and ruled them wisely for fifty years. His final battle was with the fearsome fire dragon and happened in this way.

One day, one of Beowulf's servants ran away because he was in trouble. Looking for somewhere to hide, he accidentally discovered a remote burial mound on a rocky cliff above the sea. The servant stepped inside. As his eyes adjusted to the darkness, he made out a faint light glimmering in the distance. He moved toward it but stopped in his tracks as he realized it was the fiery glow from a dragon's nostrils.

The creature lay fast asleep upon a bed of golden rings, goblets, and bowls, surrounded by a glittering heap of silver swords, jewel-encrusted helmets, and coins. Thinking that just one piece of the treasure would buy him out of trouble, the servant stole a golden goblet. He crept silently from the mound and ran back home with it as fast as he could.

When the dragon awoke that night, it immediately noticed that it had been robbed. Angered, the fire-breathing monster swept down from the mound to take its revenge. It flew the length and breadth of Beowulf's kingdom, setting fire to villages and farms.

Although Beowulf was now an old man, he realized that he must try to rid his people of the terrible fire dragon.

With a small band of warriors, Beowulf set out for the burial mound, led by the disgraced servant. As they drew near, Wiglaf, the youngest in the group, begged to go and fight alongside his king, but Beowulf chose to face the dragon alone. At the entrance, Beowulf called out, "Dragon, come forth and face your destroyer!" He raised his iron shield against the dragon's flames and charged toward his enemy. The old king struck out with his sword, but the blade just bounced off the dragon's horny head. Beowulf's face was blackened by fire and his hair stood ablaze. He struck again and again, but the sword cracked and then shattered in his hands. He reached for his dagger, but he was too late to prevent the dragon's poisonous fangs from ripping at his neck. Just then young Wiglaf rushed to the king's side and jabbed his sword into the flesh below the monster's jaws. Immediately the dragon's fire weakened.

Together, Beowulf and Wiglaf hacked at the dragon's hide until the beast collapsed before them and died. But in those few moments the poison had taken hold of the old king's life. Anxious to please him, young Wiglaf ran into the mound and brought out armfuls of the dragon's treasure.

As his life slipped away, Beowulf gave his own helmet and golden ring to Wiglaf. With his last breath he told his bravest follower, "Now you shall take my place as king of the Geats."

SAINT GEORGE

Saint George was born in Eastern Turkey about 1,700 years ago. This story about him was told to demonstrate the power of Christianity over evil. It was first written down in the sixth century.

George was a Roman soldier in the Emperor's Imperial Guard. When the emperor passed a law stating that all Christians should be killed, George was horrified. He immediately left the Roman army and took up the Christian faith himself. George traveled back to his birthplace, Cappadocia, in Turkey.

He put on a suit of silver armor with the sign of the Cross on his buckle and shield. Then, riding a horse draped in gold, George set out to seek adventure and spread the Christian faith.

It so happened that a monstrous dragon was on the rampage in the Libyan city of Silene. It had come down from the bleak hills and made its home in a large lake on the outskirts of the city.

The dragon fed on the sheep and cattle that grazed on the hills. Then one day the mangled remains of a shepherd boy were found. From that time on, the dragon came right up to the city gates in its search for food. Soon the only way to keep it away was to leave two sheep every day by the lake. But after a while there were no sheep left to give the dragon.

The city council met and came to a dreadful decision. The dragon would have to be fed with children. Names would be picked each day to see which child should be left beside the dragon's lake. One day the lot fell to the king's daughter. He pleaded for her life, but it was no use. The princess, dressed like a bride, was tied to a rock near the dragon's lake.

As the princess was waiting for the dragon to claim her, George rode by on his horse. He prepared to rescue her, but she told him to pass by or the dragon would kill him too. George refused to go. He said, "In the name of Jesus Christ, I shall save you from this dragon!" And he rode down to the water's edge. When the huge, scaly monster emerged, George steadied his horse and charged at the dragon. In one forceful thrust his lance penetrated the beast's belly. Immediately the dragon stopped fighting. George told the princess to tie her silken belt around the dragon's neck, and together they led it back to the city.

The people of Silene were amazed to see the wounded dragon. George told them that it was Christ the Lord who had delivered them from evil. The king and all his people were baptized into the Christian faith, and George chopped off the dragon's head. It took four cartloads to carry the monster's bloody remains from the city.

Some say George married the princess. According to history, he was later tortured and killed for his faith. But 800 years after his death, when Christianity began to flower, George was made a saint.

THE LAMBTON WORM

This folktale lives on in Worm Hill and Worm Well—
areas in County Durham, England.

The heir to Lambton Hall was a lazy and irresponsible fellow who liked nothing better than to fish for salmon in the Wear River. One Sunday, when everyone else was at church, Lambton hooked an evil-looking worm from the river. "It looks like the devil itself," said a passing stranger. But on his way home Lambton tossed the worm down the village well and thought no more about it.

The years passed. Young Lambton grew out of his idle ways and left home to fight in the Holy Crusades. Meanwhile, still hidden at the bottom of the well, the worm had continued to grow. One day, to the horror of the villagers, the terrible worm crawled out of the well and made its way to the Wear River. By day it wound itself around a rock in the water, and at night it slept coiled ten times around a neighboring hill. As it grew ever larger, the worm became the terror of the countryside, with a hideous hunger for man, milk, and beast. One day it crossed the Wear River to Lambton Hall. But, following the advice of the head servant, the household was prepared. The largest horse trough in the castle yard had been filled to the brim with milk. The worm drank its fill of the milk and slithered away.

Every day it came back to the castle for more milk. If there was one drop less than usual, the wicked worm would wind its tail around the trees and tear them from the ground.

The household suffered seven years of this daily ritual. Then young Lambton returned home from the wars. He realized with dismay that this was the same worm he had thrown down the well years before. So he went to the local witch for advice. She told him to go and fight the worm, wearing a suit of armor studded with spikes. She added that once the worm was dead, Lambton must kill the next living creature he saw. Otherwise a terrible curse would fall upon his entire family.

Lambton did just as he was told. As the worm wound itself around him, his armor started to crack, but the spikes sank into the creature's flesh and its blood gushed forth. As the worm squeezed ever more tightly, its body was cut apart. Piece by piece, it fell into the rushing river. When only the head remained, the worm's eyes flashed fiercely at Lambton before vanishing in the water. Lambton looked up—and to his horror the first living creature he saw was his father. Of course he could not kill his own father, so the next nine generations of the Lambton family were doomed to die in battle or abroad, but never at home. The awful worm had its revenge after all.

THE MORDIFORD WYVERN

A wyvern was a two-legged dragon with wings. Records from 1607 mention
a painting of a wyvern in the church at Mordiford, a village in England.
People in Mordiford tell this dragon folktale.

 Maud was a child who loved to wander in the woods near her home and make friends with wild animals. One day she discovered a strange animal lying fast asleep in the woodland grass. It was no bigger than a cucumber, with folded wings and skin that sparkled. Maud gently touched the tiny creature, which instantly fluttered into the air. After many attempts, she managed to lure it down with a saucer of milk. The baby wyvern—for that is what it was—licked the saucer clean and then crawled affectionately into her arms. Unaware of what she had found, Maud took the creature home. When her father saw it, he became fearful and told Maud to put the creature back where she had found it. But Maud disobeyed and kept her pet secretly in a small cage in the yard behind the house.

Each day as Maud innocently fed the wyvern milk, its evil nature grew. Before long it broke out of its cage and flew back to the woods. At first the wyvern lived on rabbits and squirrels, but soon it grew fond of cattle and sheep. Then one day it devoured a plump young shepherd boy as he slept beside his sheep.

Day by day, as more lives were taken, the villagers feared for themselves and their families. The only person who seemed safe was Maud, perhaps because the wyvern remembered her kindness. But even Maud became afraid as the monster kept on killing.

Each attempt to destroy the dragon was a failure, until one day a prisoner named Garston offered to try. He was condemned to die, but the judge promised to free him if he could rid Mordiford of the terrible monster.

Garston built a barrel that he spiked with deadly hooks and blades. He placed the barrel in the wyvern's path and crawled inside. As the wyvern came near, it stopped. The smell of human flesh made the monster start to drool.

The dragon coiled its powerful flanks around the spiky container. With all its strength, it tried to crush the barrel to get at Garston. The harder it squeezed, the more blood poured from beneath its scaly skin. Inside, Garston felt hot and breathless. Through a peephole he could see the wounded wyvern's fiery breath set fire to the bushes and trees nearby.

Suddenly the barrel began to crack. Garston began firing his pistol through the peephole. The wyvern writhed in pain, uncoiled, and fell to the ground. Convinced he had won, Garston jumped from the barrel and began to hack off the monster's head. But as he chopped, he sucked in the last poisonous fumes from the wounded dragon's breath and fell, lifeless. Garston was dead, but so was the wyvern. It would never again frighten the villagers of Mordiford.

THE GAOLIANG BRIDGE

Like many Chinese dragons, the one in this story rules over water
and is able to change its shape at will.

 Centuries ago in China, in the place where the city of Beijing now stands, the land was poor and marshy. A powerful dragon and his family ruled over the marsh, and this land belonged to them.

The Ming emperor wanted to build a great city. He decided to build it on the dragon's land. He was encouraged in his plan by a god named Nocha.

The dragon watched angrily as workers began to build the new city. In revenge, the dragon decided to deprive its people of all their precious sources of water. He changed himself and his wife into a harmless old man and old woman with a handcart containing two large water jars. Then he arranged to appear before the emperor in a dream.

As the emperor slept, the old man and old woman came to him. They asked him for permission to take their jars out of the city. Unaware that the jars contained all the waters of the entire region, the emperor said, "Of course. Take the jars with my blessing."

When the emperor woke the next morning, he heard people crying out that all through the kingdom the water supply had completely dried up.

The god Nocha understood what had happened. He was unable to stop the dragons from appearing to the emperor in a dream, but he himself appeared in a dream to Liu Bowen, the chief builder of the city. In the dream, Nocha told Liu Bowen what he must do to bring back the missing water.

First Liu Bowen sent messengers to all the city gates to find out who had left the city during the night. When he learned that the old man and old woman had taken their handcart out through the west gate, he knew he had to act quickly. The road to the west was the road that led to the sea. The jars had to be destroyed before the dragons reached the sea, where the city's water would be lost forever.

Liu Bowen asked for a brave soldier to volunteer for the dangerous task. Only one stepped forward. His name was Gaoliang. Liu Bowen handed Gaoliang a lance with which to break the jars. "Catch up with the cart as silently as you can," he said. "Pierce both jars and return quickly to the city. Do not turn around. Do not look back!"

Gaoliang took the lance and sped away.

Soon he spotted the dragons in their disguise. Slowly he crept up close and shattered one of the jars. But before he could break the other one, the water from the first gushed out with such force that it threatened to drown him. At the same moment, a thunderous crash rippled through the sky as the old man transformed himself back into a dragon. Although his task was only half complete, Gaoliang had no choice but to flee back to the city.

The roar and rumble of the gushing water followed Gaoliang all the way home. As he neared the city gates, Gaoliang felt he must be safe. Then he saw Liu Bowen staring at what lay behind him. Gaoliang forgot his orders and turned around. A huge wave swept over him and he was drowned.

A bridge was built just outside the city in honor of the soldier who so bravely tried to save it. The Gaoliang Bridge stood for centuries.

The jar that Gaoliang did not shatter was said to hold all the city's sweet spring water. Thereafter, sweet water was found only in the hills where Gaoliang caught up with the dragon. The place is called the Hill of Jade Springs. But the water that came back to the city from the broken jar has remained bitter, even to this day.

THE CHINESE DRAGON'S PEARL

A Chinese dragon carried a bright pearl of great power and value under its chin or inside its throat.

 Long ago in China, a young boy and his mother lived by the banks of the Min River. The boy earned what little money he could by cutting fresh grass and selling it to the villagers for their animals.

One summer there was no rain. The boy had to travel farther and farther to find grass that wasn't dry and brown. At last, many miles from the village, he came across a patch of lush green grass. He cut as much as he could carry and hurried all the way home to sell it.

Day after day he went back to the same place, where the grass seemed always to spring up again, strangely bright and green.

After a while the boy grew weary of so much walking. He decided to dig up some of the grass and plant it near his home. He took a spade and dug himself a nice square of turf.

To his great surprise, when he lifted the earth,
an enormous gleaming pearl rolled out!
The boy pocketed the pearl, shouldered his
spade, and carefully carried home his square
of grass. He planted the grass, and then he showed
the pearl to his mother.

"This pearl is worth a great deal of money," she said and
hid it for safekeeping in an almost empty rice jar.

The next morning the boy was saddened to find that his grass had
shriveled up and died.

"Never mind," said his mother. "Our pearl will buy us food." And she
opened the lid of the rice jar. To her amazement, it was brimming with
grains of rice. She looked at her son. Both of them realized at once that
the pearl was magic. So that night they placed the pearl on top of the
last three coins in their money jar. By morning the jar was full of bright,
shiny coins.

The boy and his mother told no one about the pearl, but soon it
became obvious to other people that they were growing richer and
richer. One day robbers broke into the house. The boy looked
on in horror as they came close to the pearl's hiding place.
In panic he grabbed the pearl from the jar, popped it
into his mouth, and swallowed it! As the pearl
made its way down to the boy's belly, his
insides began to burn.

He ran to the nearby well and poured whole buckets of water down his throat, but still the fire raged. He rushed to the river and gulped down more water. Then, before his mother's eyes, the boy began to swell up. His body trembled. His skin cracked and got scaly. He sprouted horns and wings. In moments the boy had become a dragon.

As the new dragon dived into the river, the heavens opened and rain poured onto the dried-up land. The horrified mother cried out to her lost son. Frantically he twisted and turned to look back at her. The great coils of his scaly body lashed back and forth in the rushing water, causing mud from the bottom of the river to be pushed up into huge banks. The mudbanks are still there today. They are known as the "Looking Back at Mother" banks.

DRAGONS AROUND THE WORLD

Hundreds of fantastic dragons appear in the stories of most cultures from around the world. As the pictures in this book illustrate, not all dragons have four legs, clawed feet, and wings: They come in many different sizes, shapes, and colors. They can be part of local folklore or a national legend. Sometimes they are known from an isolated report in church records or in an early scientist's notes. Here are just a few of the better known types.

The Amphiptère (America, North Africa, Europe)

Amphiptères were legless winged dragons, or flying serpents. They were first seen in ancient Egypt, guarding the frankincense trees in great swarms. A beautiful account describes them in the woods around Penllyne Castle in Wales. They had eyes like the feathers in a peacock's tail and wings that sparkled and glittered wherever they flew.

The Piasa (North America)

The Algonquin Indians of North America worshiped a dragon with the face of a man and a tail that was twice as long as a man is tall. An ancient painting of the dragon, thought to be "life-sized," once existed on Piasa Rock in Illinois, but it was unfortunately blown up by workers quarrying for stone. In the Algonquins' native language, *piasa* means "man-eating bird."

The O-Gon-Cho (Japan)

The O-Gon-Cho was a white dragon that lived in a deep pond at Yamashiro. Every fifty years the dragon rose from the pond and flew as a golden-feathered bird. Its howl warned the people that disaster was coming.

The Ethiopian Dream (Africa)

This dragon had four wings and clawed feet. It was large enough to kill elephants and often ate poisonous plants that made its bite more deadly. Four or five of these dragons were once reported to have twisted themselves together like willow tree branches and sailed across the sea to find fresh food supplies in Arabia.

The Tarasque (France)

The Tarasque was half-fish, half-animal. It lived in a forest near the Rhône River, where it sank boats and devoured the passengers. The local inhabitants prayed to Saint Martha, who was famous for performing miracles. Saint Martha held out her cross before the Tarasque and sprinkled it with holy water. Cowering before such forces for Good, the Tarasque was led to a nearby village, now named Tarascon, where it was put to death by the villagers.

The Amphisbaena (Africa)

This dragon had a head at each end and could move in either direction. While a female Amphisbaena's eggs were hatching, she could keep one head at a time awake to watch over them. Today there is a South American lizard that gives the impression of having two heads. When threatened, it raises its tail and moves backward and forward.

The Midgard Serpent (Scandinavia)

The Midgard Serpent of Scandinavian mythology was so long that it slept in the sea with its tail in its mouth and its body encircling the entire world. According to the myth, Midgard will wake at the end of the world and be killed by Thor, god of war and thunder, who will also die in the struggle.

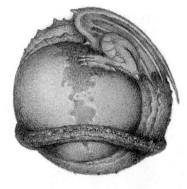

The Chinese Dragon, or *Lung* (China)

Chinese dragons laid their eggs on the banks of rivers or lakes. The eggs looked like beautiful stones and took a thousand years to hatch.

When the first crack appeared in an egg, the parents each cried out. The father's cry whipped up the winds, and the mother's cry calmed them. Lashing rain and booming thunder rocked the world as the egg burst open and the young dragon was born. It took fifteen hundred years to become a full-grown *lung*, another five hundred to grow horns, and a thousand more to develop wings.

There were four main kinds of *lung*: the Tien-lung (celestial dragon), which held high the palaces of the gods; the Shen-lung (spiritual dragon), which controlled the wind and rain; the Ti-lung (earth dragon), which ruled the rivers and streams; and the Fut's-lung (underground dragon), which guarded precious metals and treasure.

Dragon Poem

by H. D. C. Peplar (1916)

Child

Are all the dragons fled?
Are all the goblins dead?
Am I quite safe in bed?

Nurse

Thou art quite safe in bed,
Dragons and goblins all are dead.

Child

When Michael's angels fought
The dragon, was it caught,
Did it jump and roar,
(Oh Nurse, don't shut the door),
And did it try to bite?
(Nurse, don't blow out the light.)

Nurse

Hush, thou knowest what I said,
Saints and dragons all are dead.

Father (to himself)

O Child, Nurse lies to thee,
For dragons thou shalt see,
Please God that on that day,
Thou may'st a dragon slay,
And if thou dost not faint,
God shall not want a Saint.

INDEX